I0677841

# Island Pieces

## Jeremy Luke Hill

Vocamus Press
Guelph, Ontario

Written by Jeremy Luke Hill
Some rights reserved
©①⊜◎

Cover Photograph by Jeremy Luke Hill
Some rights reserved
©①⊜◎

ISBN 13: 978-0-9880176-3-4 (hbk)
ISBN 13: 978-0-9880176-4-1 (pbk)
ISBN 13: 978-0-9880176-5-8 (ebk)

Vocamus Press
130 Dublin Street, North
Guelph, Ontario, Canada
N1H 4N4

www.vocamus.net

2012

To my brothers, who were there.

# Contents

# Preface

I started writing this collection in bits and pieces more than twenty years ago, when I was still going to Manitoulin Island with my father and brothers for several weeks each summer, living at my Grandfather Gordon's hunting camp near Carter Bay, and visiting my Grandfather Hill's farm outside of Mindemoya. Our time there was mostly our own, the kind of time that occurs only in childhood, and even then only when it is allowed the freedom truly to be childhood, the kind of time, vast and undefined, that persists in the memory as vague sensation and brilliant image, as dream and fantasy, more imagination than memory. We read and played, fished and swam, mowed hay and milked cows, but mostly, at least in my imagined memory, we wandered, through woods and along creeks and over fence lines and down dirt roads and under bridges and across the great exposed rocks of the island. We picked our way through the landscape, unaware that we were becoming changed by it, that it was becoming the definitive landscape that would call to us across the coming years, even when we had settled ourselves apart from it.

I had no formal language at the time to describe what I was writing, so I referred to the pieces I wrote as reflections, but I would now call them prose poems, perhaps, or near enough. They were generally short, inspired by something immediate, jotted on loose leaf pages in the earlier years and then later in journals as I began to be more deliberate about keeping track of them. Most of the earliest examples, those on loose leaf, have since been lost, but I can remember many of them, not as finished pieces, but as images and impressions, as isolated words and phrases that drift like ghosts among the later attempts that I have collected here. It is as if, and there is something more than metaphor in this for me, I have been writing new words over the old ones, the later words obscuring but not quite effacing those beneath them, so that none of the pieces are separable any longer, so that they are all a part of each other and part of that childhood that I must have lived, but that I can now only imagine, and that comes to be, in the words I write, something that I could not even have imagined.

I returned often to these pieces over the years, adding and revising and combining, and some of them gradually took on new forms, poems or stories, and these too I continued to edit and rework, never in any serious way, but never idly either. They were like habitual walking paths, always changing but always familiar also, places where I could wander unhurried, revisiting and retracing, marking my way through them as I passed. It was not just that they were reminders of my childhood and my youth, though this was certainly part of their appeal. It was also that they returned me to the landscape of the north in ways that became increasingly significant to my imagination, returned me to places where life clings tenuously to a thin skiff of earth that hardly covers the shield rock, where living things seem merely afterthoughts to stone and water and sky. There seemed to me something profoundly true in this, something that remained true even when I was living where the soil had gathered more deeply or where the pavement had hidden the soil altogether, and so I was often drawn back to what I had written of this northern landscape, continually reshaping those long-ago words.

As more and more of these pieces developed into stories, I began to play with the idea of making a collection of them, but many of the original reflections would not lend themselves to the length of a short story, and yet they were so intimately connected to the creation of the longer pieces that I could not bring myself to remove them from the collection entirely. I struggled with this problem for quite some time before realizing, what should have been obvious from the beginning, that there was nothing preventing me from combining the longer stories and the shorter reflections together, nor, for that matter, from including poetry and photography as well. The collection then began to take shape fairly quickly, and I was pleased with the effect of having a variety of genres and styles in combination. It seemed a more accurate reflection of my experience, of how the island had inspired me sometimes in one way and sometimes in another, of how some things had grown over the years while other things had remained much as they first were. I only hope that my readers will find the eclecticism as appealing as I do.

I should also mention, by way of warning, that though some of these pieces are drawn as faithfully from my memory as possible, my memory is anything but faithful, and in many cases, especially in the longer stories, what began as memory, has become something quite different over years of continual rewriting. These pieces do not represent anything like historical accuracy. They represent only what I first lived and wrote and then remembered and rewrote and then imagined and rewrote again. That is all.

I have dedicated the collection to my brothers, since they were with me through many of the experiences that informed it, but there are many others to whom it should be dedicated as well: to my father, who took the five of us to the island each summer; to my mother, with whom my own children are coming to experience the island landscape for themselves; to my grandparents, who endured our noise, our roughhousing, and our unending appetites with remarkable grace; and to the many friends and relatives who left their marks on our island summers.

# Cutting Trail

It is early yet, but I wake, smelling cedar and woodsmoke and old mattresses and mosquito repellent, the smell of the camp, the fire, the forest, all of it, still the smell of summer to me now, all these years later, and I am lying in the top-right bunk, my head closest to the window, its pane already cracked on the morning I am imagining, broken now. The sun is just rising, and the crack in the glass glistens like frozen lightning, and everything is quiet, not completely, with birds singing and squirrels dropping pine cones from the canopy and trees swaying in the breeze and coals popping in the woodstove, but profoundly, because these sounds do not break the silence so much as they deepen it, make it a mystery. The sun finds its way between the log walls, between its upright cedars, peeled and knotty and chinked with cement that is crumbling away, leaving holes for the wind and for

9

the cold but also for the light, weak still and diffused, that finds its way through the mortar and speckles my sleeping bag in patches of lighter green that drift with infinite patience.

I can hear the others beginning to stir, and I slip to the floor, into the cool, trying not to wake the younger ones. My clothes are hanging on the bookshelf, as near as possible to the black, rust-ringed ventpipe of the wood-stove. They are as warm as my bed was, and all the warmer because I have just plunged into the cold of the forest-shadowed, still-darkened morning, my bare feet on the chill of the linoleum with its coal-melted pockmarks, because I have just shed my shirt and shorts, sleep-warm, to feel the morning more keenly. I am tempted to stand there a moment, prolong the chill and the expectation of warmth together, but the day promises too much, and I am too eager, and I turn to where my clothes hang on the roughcut bookshelf.

I helped make the bookshelf when I was just a child, watched the pine trees being felled and then sat on the back of the old tractor as it pulled the log waggon from the camp up Jerry Co. Road and Timber Bay Road and Carter Bay Road and then along the few hundred yards of Government Road to Lentir's sawmill, heavy with the smell of diesel and engine oil and conifer. The logs went through the sawblade, pass after pass, and the planks fell, mostly bark at first, but thicker soon, the sawdust pluming upward and then settling in fragrant piles. I watched as the men stacked the furred boards, marked with the sawblade's half-moon scars, piled them on the waggon, left them waiting to be joined by mismatched nails, some heads broader than others, some steel and some brass, driven on angles that split the wood, but the shelf they became holds books just the same, and it keeps my clothes close to the stove.

It was on this bookshelf that I caught a mouse once, with my bare hands. I was sitting in the old armchair, the one that used to be my grandfather's favourite chair, but had become his camp chair, slowly disintegrating, year by year, taking root next to the woodstove. My coffee was on the bookshelf, my feet on a length of firewood set upright, close to the stove, and I was reading something, I no longer remember what. I looked up for my cup, saw the mouse from the corner of my eye, and it froze where it was, along one of the bookshelf's vertical edges, halfway between two shelves, so that we were eye to eye. I laid my book on the floor, and I put one hand below the mouse, only an inch or so from his head. It turned around then, quickly, so I put my other hand above it, trapping it along its narrow path, and I took it by its tail, held it close to my eyes, looked at it as nearly as I could, watched its forepaws swim, not frantically, but with a perfect nonchalance, until I took it outside and dashed its head against a tree, threw its body into the woods.

On the morning I am imagining, however, that other

morning, the profoundly quiet morning, there is only my warming clothes on the bookshelf, and I dress alongside my brothers, our voices, whispered and sporadic, fulfilling the stillness of everything, establishing its vastness through our insignificance. We have not lit the lamps, only stoked the fire in the stove, so we dress and pack in the dimness of the firelight and in the suggestion of a still invisible sun, a light that appears only as lightning in a broken window and as patches of colour that drift through holes in the wall.

We cook eggs and bacon in the cast iron pan, bacon first, crisping in its own drippings, then eggs on top, roughly scrambled into the grease and into the now crumbled bacon. The coffee is perking on the stove too, popping, softly popping, and we say nothing as we pull our chairs close to the woodstove's open door to warm ourselves as we eat. The coals burn red in the draft, and the new wood blackens and flames, and it feels like the stove is the centre of everything, not just of the three of us who are eating around it, not just of the cabin that it warms against the cool of the forest, but of everything, the world and the universe and everything. This is what the fireplace means, I think, it means the centre, the place where you begin and end.

It is this centre that we will soon leave behind as we close the too-wide screen door, softly, so as not to wake the others with its characteristic bang, though I hear the bang anyway, because I have opened and closed that door too many times, because I have heard it screech as it opens and slam as it closes too many times, and I can no longer hear one without the other. The screech of any screen door now, no matter how distant, is always the screech of that wooden camp screen, with its diagonal board running between too-distant corners, and my mind always follows the screech with a slam, so I hear it slam that morning, though we do not forget to close it softly, and it sounds like a finality, like we are being cut off from the fire at the centre, at least for a time, and I feel this as exhilaration.

We enter the forest at the back of the cabin, between the old tractor and the outhouse, though I cannot now find the spot exactly, not after the scrub plants have had so many years to grow, and not after the tractor has been moved over beside the new winterized cabin, its crankcase engine refusing ever to die completely and its chassis repainted until it is immune to rust, and not after the outhouse has slumped and toppled, its particle board chewed by porcupines and rotted by damp. Too much time has passed. The marks we made were too ephemeral. We set out that day, passing between the tractor and the outhouse, to cut a path, to blaze a trail, but all signs of our passing have themselves now passed, and I cannot find our blazes, though my search is diligent. The world does not remember like I do. Its memories are overgrown, while mine are stark, barren, like solitary trees on a wide plain, and what stands on the plains of

that morning is the instant, only just an instant, when
we pause beneath the eaves of the forest and let the trail,
not yet a trail, but soon to be a trail, choose for us where
it will be, the instant when we feel its need, like a living
thing, to be. Not just because the road to the lake, the
usual one, is circuitous, first winding away from the lake,
through the woods along Jerry Co. Road, just a set of
tracks, split by grass and devil's paintbrushes and but-
tercups, bordered by raspberry canes and dogwood and
sumac, and then spilling out onto the logging road that
runs along the hundred acre woodlots toward Carter Bay
Road, then another two or three kilometers more to the
beach, and not just because the new trail will be more
direct, straight through the bush to the beach, a walking
trail at first, then broader and clearer each time, firm,
direct, from camp to beach, but also because the trail
simply needs to be, because our willingness to make it
has breathed into it a spirit that now requires a form.
This is what stands in my memory, the trail's need to
be, a lonely and aching need now that it is only a mem-
ory, but an intimate and insistent need then, as we stand
before it, hesitate, and are pulled along by it, into it.

We bring with us the machete that we discovered in
the woodshed that summer, its handle wrapped in cloth
tape and stained with rust along the blade, a wicked
looking thing, so that we hardly dared pick it up when
we first found it, just looked at one another to see if it
had affected us all with the same dread, and then looked

back at the menace of it, the bloodiness of it, though we knew rust from blood. It was brought to the camp by one of our uncles, we supposed, or maybe by one of their hunting friends, but it was clearly unclaimed, lying there rusting in the shed, so we cleaned it and oiled it, sharpened it with the whetstone, replaced the tape on the handle, all the while telling stories about it, until it had become something mythical, hovering somewhere between the sacred and the profane, a gift from nameless gods of no firm allegiance.

We bring the limbing axe too, a hatchet head mounted on a full-length handle, deeply worn and darkly stained around the grip, having somehow survived its first axe head, as few handles do, and now whittled down to fit the hatchet head, becoming the limbing axe, longer than the hatchet, lighter than the logging axe, slenderer than the splitting maul, perfect for trimming branches from felled trees or cutting roasting sticks.

I carry the pack first, while the other two wield the machete and the hatchet, one clearing the brush, the other felling small saplings and obstructing limbs. The machete makes a swishing sound, punctuated by sharp pings, through leaves and stems, swish-ping-swish-ping-ping-swish. It flickers in the growing sunlight, a rhythmic flash to accompany its rhythmic sound, and it leaves the ground stubbled and bristled like an unshaven face, and the hatchet follows, treading the stubble of the machete underfoot, cutting more deeply into the stuff of the forest, taking the limbs and the saplings, mostly cedar and pine, leaving them to line the path and to scent the air with pitch, like incense hallowing a sacred procession.

The cuts we make are deep, we think, deep enough to make a lasting wound through the forest, to make a trail of blood that can be followed, something to be reopened again and again, to be packed with ash or horsehair until the scar has formed: a ritual scar, a duelling scar, to show where we have passed, what we have done, badges of honour that we inflict on the body of the forest. We do not merely blaze a trail, we emblazon the flesh of the forest, claim it, make it one of us through the scars of our tribe, through the mutual drawing of blood, for we receive wounds as well as give them, take our mensur marks with the necessary courage, with the requisite indifference, as falling boughs and tangled thorns and stinging nettles trade us mark for mark, badge for badge, brand for brand.

We are enraptured by the still open wounds we are making, cannot imagine a future, not of any kind, certainly not one where we will come looking for traces of the blows we strike today, where we will need those traces, search for them, and not find them, where we will wonder whether the stumps have been covered by forest litter and the severed limbs hidden by new grown branches, or whether we are looking in the wrong places, because the marks that seemed so telling have disappeared now. We cannot imagine that this thing we are making, this spirit taking on flesh, this need drawing us forward, this presence becoming fuller and heavier in our wake, will ever be anything than it is now. It will always be in this moment of becoming, always bleeding itself into being.

I first knew the blood of trees like this when I watched the maple sap drip down spigots into tin pails in the sugar bush behind my grandfather's farm, thinking that the bleeding of the sap, drop by drop – pling, pling, pling – into the empty bucket, and then deeper, hollower – plink, plunk, plonk – as is it filled, that this bleeding made the tree real, made it be. The maples were still just waking into spring, still just dry bones awaiting the flesh of leaves, but their blood flowed in them, flowed from far beneath the snow-patched ground to grant each branch a veil of the goldest green to set against the cloud-patched sky, and I stood there to see the drops collect, like the blood that had dripped from my brother's arm when he fell and broke the bone so that it punctured the skin, and we helped him home with those same drops falling behind us at every step, and it was unalterably true then, looking into the pail, that everything real must bleed, that only blood makes something truly be, and the pail of sap became suddenly sacrificial, like a cup held to catch the last life of a dying God.

The path behind us is hallowed by the blood we have spilled, sanctifying the earth, making it holy ground, so that we could not turn back if we wanted, not without taking off our shoes and tearing our clothes and putting ashes in our hair, not without consenting to go on our knees, our hands clasped before us like pilgrims on a sacred way, mopping up the blood of trees with cloths to be the relics of some future faith. We are no longer worthy to return that way, because it is our sin, our violence, that has made it holy.

At last, how soon, the sun rises above the trees, and the dawn chill disappears, all at once, between breaths, melting the pitch of pine and balsam so that it smears our blades and coats our hands, collects needles and flakes of bark to rub our skin to blisters. The dew evaporates, thick and clinging, mixes with the sweat that no longer cools but paints our skin in streaks of dirt that collect in the corners of our eyes and the creases of our bodies. Everything has changed, between one blow and the next, and we are staggered by this new and sudden forest, humid and calescent, swarmed by deer flies, swift and relentless. We stop often now, every time we trade places, exchange pack for machete, machete for hatchet, hatchet for pack, and the pack, once a burden and a nuisance, becomes a relief from the labour of the trail, lightening with every stop, as the water is shared around, diminishing far too quickly. The ground keeps opening into meadows now, thin grasses growing in the crevices of the shield rock, a hatch of grasses across the lichen-covered stone, like a miniature landscape of fields and hedgerows, so we must mark the path as we can, drag fallen logs from the forest, move what stones can be moved, and all the

while there is the sun and the sun-heated rock, and we
have not, as best we can guess, gone even a third of our
way, though the sun is high enough for us to eat what
food we have brought, sheltering in the shade of a birch
stand.

We have misjudged. We did not scar the forest, only
forced ourselves a little way from its womb, from the
frozen lightning and the drifting green sunlight and the
gentle fire at its centre, and now we are infants, crawl-
ing about in a world we could not have expected. We are
not inflicting the trail on the forest. We are clinging to it,
like an umbilical cord stretching bloody and white-blue
behind us, or like Ariadne's thread, unspooling through
labyrinthine fears, or like the cord tied around the ankles
of priests, to drag their bodies from the holy of holies if
they should anger their God and be struck down. We
dangle on the end of the trail, our weight holding it taut
behind us, and our greatest fear now is that it will break,
be eaten up like a trail of bread crumbs, leave us unteth-
ered to face whatever monsters or gods await us.

The thread of the trail grows tighter and tighter be-
hind us, fraying and unravelling as our arms tire, as we
allow ourselves to weave now, between trees and around
meadows, taking the path of least resistance, scarcely
breaking the skin of the forest, and still, we can only
be perhaps two thirds of the way to the lake. We take
off our shirts and wrap them in awkward bandages over
our raw and blistered hands, and our bodies, pale still

so early in the summer, are soon sun-red and scratched, smeared with pitch and pine needles, traced with lines of sweat and dirt, as if the forest is writing its story on our skin, leaving its icons and hieroglyphs, fearful scripts, intelligible only to itself, but surely the language of some primordial magic.

On other days I will walk beneath those same trees, quite apart from any trail, and the forest will move me, and I will write about the dogwood shooting up from the litter, the scrambling junipers, the saplings of spruce and balsam, the birch and cedar, and I will write that they make the sky stand vertical, that they rupture its vastness, trouble its expanse, urge it still higher to the terror of its beyond, and I will write that their limbs are like roots burrowing into a blue, thin, transparent soil, their trunks suspended above a green, impenetrable sky, adrift between two heavens and two earths, surrounded by long shadows, sun-flung and invisible, their branches becoming roots that are cast, insubstantial, into earthen skies, and I will write that the sun strikes down through them to touch the ground and grant each branch and leaf its halo all of gold, but on that day we are unmoved. It is a far different forest that we walk, a forest of stern will and fearful incantations that tolerates us only for a time, inscribes itself on our bodies, drives us through its sacred places, covers our traces almost as soon as we have passed.

It is into this forest that the sun begins to cast itself,

so soon, before we have reached our end, touching lightly the tops of the trees to our left, and we know that we have failed, that the trail will not find the lake, will not link the cabin to the beach with a sure, straight line, not on this day or on any other. The sun sets as finally as the slam of a screen door, and something finds release in us, as if the line that tethered us has been cut by it, as if we are no longer bound to make our scars, no longer tethered to the womb or to the one who holds the thread or to the ones who wait to pull us from the inner sanctuary. We have been loosed into whatever awaits us, and we no longer walk but run, dodging and tripping and stumbling and running, for it seems to us that we can make out the blue of the water through the trunks of the trees, a blue that has been revealed only by the setting sun, and it calls us, though it is still a long way off, calls us, as surely as the trail has driven us.

It has us by the ears and nostrils now, drags us by sound and smell as much as by sight, the water-blue, there, somewhere beneath the sky-blue, there, between the crowding trees, there again, and broader now, nearer and more certain, a rolling-and-crowned-with-white-blue, a curling-and-traced-with-green-blue, through the last of the cedars and over the pitted stones, it casts our things aside, tears our clothes from us, and seizes us at last.

# Through Unmarked Time

She paused on the topmost stair,
as if she had found, without expectation,
a place preordained for her,
and the sun dappling through the cedars,
and the lake breeze stirring her clothing,
welcomed her like a long expected mistress,
and she turned back toward the sun,
eyes closed and face lifted,
innocent of the face also lifted to her,
the gaze that passed over her
like the sun and like the breeze,
and her pause grew to a waiting,
and his waiting to a stillness,
and the sun's stillness to an eternity,
a caress through unmarked time.

# A Hill By The Harbour

The hill, raising its stones from the harbour, is left to nature, to the scrambling cedars and to the northern scrub plants, dogwood and sumac and creeping juniper, finding purchase here or there, but the heights have all been claimed by cottages, claimed long enough ago that their lawns now imitate their more southern and more suburban counterparts, so the trees are much fewer, if mostly cedar still, and the brush has vanished altogether, and the trees that do remain stand with their lower trunks bare, so that they seem to wade with their skirts up, long-legged in the waves of unruly foliage below them.

# An Invitation

"Will you be back for Christmas?" Her face was lowered, her hair falling straight as plumb lines.

"Probably." I leaned back against the log post of the porch, feeling its smoothness between my shoulders. "We usually do."

"You guys could come skating at our place."

I thought she would say more, but she didn't. "Sure," I said. "That would be fun." It was late enough in the afternoon that the camp was mostly shadowed in the early twilight of the forest. The cookfire was started but not yet low enough for cooking. Hotdogs wrapped in bannock were sitting on a wire rack atop the picnic table. There was a pot of beans beside them. The first mosquitoes of the evening were venturing out from their moist places.

Her eyes flashed upward, briefly, beyond the plumb

lines of her hair. "There just aren't a lot of people you can talk to around here, you know?"

I nodded, but she wasn't looking anymore, half-turned away from me, sitting on the edge of the picnic table, looking down the path toward the stream. "There aren't that many where I live either," I said.

She didn't answer for a long time. We could hear the others playing some kind of game in the forest, their shouts pinballing through the trees. "I guess I'll just have to wait, you know, for the right person to come along." She seemed to be waiting for me to reply, but I didn't know what she wanted me to say, and she went on without me. "Maybe when I'm in university."

"Yeah," I said. "Maybe."

Her mother came out of the cabin, picked up the rack of hotdogs, set them carefully over the coals, and I got up from the post, went to tend the fire.

# The Dune

The dune was taller, more fixed, more permanent than the others. Its arms formed an almost complete circle, a broad hollow opening onto the woods that bordered the beach. Snake grass grew along its crest, creeping even some ways down its sides, trapping earth in its roots and supporting small trees that sprouted like bristles down its spine. Along one arm, as it approached the woods, three large cedars had taken hold in the thin earth so that they cast their shadows into the hollow of the dune, further and further as the sun declined in the afternoon.

Below the tufting snake grass and the creeping sand plants and the tenacious cedars, there was a strip of clean white sand, like a band, below which the sand darkened suddenly, became mixed with larger pebbles, bits of drift-wood, decaying leaves and grass. This dark, earthy sand ran along the bottom of the dune, melding, at the tips of its arms, with the vegetation on its crest, so that the white sand between them formed a smooth curve, arching broadly where the dune itself was broad and narrowing to nothing as the dune's arms descended to meet the level sand, as they curved to form a hollow between them.

In this rounded hollow pooled the creek that marked the border between beach and woods before breaking for the lake, circuitously, weaving through the dunes, cutting and recutting its banks daily. The pool in the hollow, in the almost round arms of the dune, seemed perfect to me, fed with enough fresh water that it smelled clean and looked clear, but slow enough that water plants grew along its edges and fingerlings played among the branches that had been carried this far by the momentum of the stream and then been caught by the slowness of the pool, as the water gathered itself toward the lake.

I came to this place daily, to the rounded arms and the broad hollow and the gathering pool and the cedars casting their shadows into the heat of the afternoon. The curve of the white sand, in the place where it was first shaded by the cedars and where I could see the stream curling around the far arm of the dune, became to me a refuge. It was a place between places, between beach and forest, between earth and sky, between sand and water, between sun and shade, and so it was also a place of solitude, because it was not a place at all, because it was only between places.

I felt that the solitude of the dune was necessary to

it, so I always came to it in solitude, following the bed of the stream from the beach toward the forest, exploring the new path that it had carved through the sand since last I had walked it. The water, coming from the hollow to which I was going, seemed always to have something of its memory with it, so that I came with a feeling of expectation already fulfilled, a knowing in advance, like a taste of something familiar in the air. For me, the taste was of silence and aloneness, and the stream bore it, since it too had passed alone through that place, had found no one there to hear its whispering or to welcome its visitation, and so it spoke to me as it passed, promised me the smell of cedar in the afternoon sun, covenanted a blue pool awaiting me in a hollow of dark earth below an arc of white sand.

Only once did the stream break its covenant with me, betray the promise that it made of a silent and sacred hollow. Once, as I approached that fixed and permanent dune, its circling and hollowed arms, there appeared a path in the sand, its trajectory gradually nearing that of the stream until they ran side by side, two sets of footprints, a purposeful path, moving unerringly toward the dune that held the pool in the hollow between its arms. I paused in the stream, in the midst of its still whispered assurances, and I looked to where the path in the sand had climbed the dune, crushing a patch of snake grass on its crest, before disappearing beyond it. The line of the dune was stark, the green of its trees and grass against the deeper shade of the forest behind it, but violated now by the cresting footprints.

I climbed the dune on my hands and knees, felt the sun, standing very high in the sky, weighing heavily on my back and head. The traces in the sand led me to the crest, and I raised my head above the broken snake grass, and in the hollow, a couple was lying, on the white strip of sand in the middle of the dune, lying almost across from where the three tall cedars had just began to advance their shadows toward the pool.

The woman lay on her back, her eyes closed, her hair disarranged, strands covering her face, left undisturbed where the occasional breeze had placed them. On her bathing suit there were embroidered butterflies, orange and green, blue and yellow, one perched on each breast, so that the arm she had thrown over her eyes seemed to ward against them as much as the sun.

Her lover lay on his side, close to her. His skin was white, not delicately but sickly, so that even the lightness of the sand seemed dark where it clung to him. He had raised himself on one elbow, leaning his head on his hand, and the darkness of his hair hung starkly against the whiteness of his hand and of his body and of the sand. He was almost absent in his whiteness, as if only his hair and his shorts kept him from disappearing altogether.

With his free hand, he was fondling the woman beside him, and he was saying something softly to her, something that needed to be said softly despite their seclusion. The woman responded neither to his touch nor to his voice, not moving even to brush away the hair that was increasingly covering her face. She seemed impassive, not from languor, but from indifference, even as he became insistent, pulling at her flesh, misshaping her butterfly breasts, half-encircling her neck, then returning his hand swiftly beyond my sight.

She gave no recognition of his touch, neither moving nor speaking, though his hand was importunate, unremitting. Then he rolled himself onto her, removing neither his clothes nor hers, fumbling between them, his eyes closed, his hips thrusting. The woman's head tilted back, her only outward acknowledgement of his assault on her unsurrendered stillness, her unrelinquished silence. She remained otherwise unmoved, her hand still thrown across her face, now seeming to ward against him rather than the butterflies or the sun. Even her eyes lay motionless beneath their closed lids.

He fell forward onto her, so that his face was pressed to the sand as he thrust against her, white grains blending with his white skin, marking his dark hair and lashes. His pale lips moved silently, his words as absent as he was, pale, translucent, and insubstantial words.

When he had finished, he raised himself on his hands above her, his face turned from hers. He adjusted their clothing and rolled away from her, leaving a space of white sand between them. He raised his arm across his eyes, unconsciously mimicking his lover, and they lay in this way, their poses and their immobility parallel. His stillness blurred still further the line between his skin and the sand.

# The Dogwoods

The dogwoods stand among the still winter-gold grasses,
red on gold, defiant, though everything will soon succumb
to green, to fecundity, to the leaves just now budding on
the dogwood stems, to the shoots hidden beneath the
litter of the grass, and to the evergreen of the forest, the
scrambling junipers, the saplings of spruce and balsam,
the outliers of a green that will soon permit no red and
gold to mar it.

# Strewn

The rocks have been tumbled and strewn, like marbles, like huge misshapen marbles, tumbled and strewn and shaken down, lying edge to edge, a field of stepping stones, bleach-white and slate-blue and gull-gray and shell-pink and rust-orange, edge to edge, from the water to the tree-line, where the water once was, when the stones were still being tumbled and strewn and shaken down, when they were still being polished one against the other, storm and surge, freeze and thaw. I am walking along their length, on their sand smoothed surfaces, and I am watching the canyons and the abysses between them, looking for the sandcherries especially, bitter and pitted, but also for whatever else there might be, for the tiny purple-blue flowers that I cannot name, the weather-stunted potentilla, the trailing silverweed, the crinkled lichen in orange and black, the swift sharpness of a snake.

The shield rock shows beneath the stones here and there, smoothly cracked and pitted, cupping the lees of spent waves, lees become red with rock-leeched iron, cups of blood in the smooth dark stone. The broad steps of the shield rise from the rock-strewn beach to the height of the point, undercut by the waves there, so that the stone gurgles and chuckles there, like a child, as the waves spray across its face. From that height the lake will seem a quilt of blues, shelves of lighter green-blues stitched to darker gray-blues, diminishing, deepening, with strips of lightness further out, where the sandbars lie. I can see them resting on their sides, the sandbars, even from here, their faces to the shore, their backs to the caresses of the currents, like giants that have slept so long that the world has swept over them and left them buried, contented, beneath sand and water and sun.

I will see also the longer arms of the two adjacent bays reaching out into the lake, holding me in the jutting centre of their half-moon, and the sunlight, perpendicular on the distant water, will make the arms seem to move, as though, at some distant time, or perhaps not so distant, they will join their hands and hold the double bay away from the deep and the cold of the lake, hold it cupped and warm until it turns as red as the pitted cups of wave-water on the shield rock, until the sun draws its waters heavenward and leaves all of it a vast field of strewn and tumbled rocks.

# A Vertical Sky

The trees make the sky stand vertical,
the birches,
the cedars,
the spruces,
the balsams,
vertical and reaching.
They rupture its vastness,
trouble its expanse,
urge it still higher
to the terror of its beyond.

# Night Swim

"Hey, kid, hop in the back. Let Jenn have shotgun."

I nodded, tried to look nonchalant as I opened the door. The window slung the late evening sun across the cab of the truck as I dropped to the gravel. I caught just a glimpse of Jenn as she came up the driveway, her long hair and cotton sundress, both hanging loosely, then I swung into the bed of the truck. I sat on the spare tire behind the driver, my back against the rear windshield. From the corner of my eye I saw Denis lean over and pull Jenn to him with his near arm, kiss her hard on the mouth. His far hand slid up under her dress between her thighs. I turned away, looked out into the almost dark, at the trees growing closely by the road, the pale length of the gravel driveway, the glow of the porch light.

The truck shifted into drive with a heavy lurch, and I steadied myself against the side. The paint was light green, like olives, dented and rusted and scratched. I glanced back through the rear window. Denis was driving with one hand. The other had pulled Jenn's dress up on her thighs, her legs showing whitely in the darkness. I looked away again. Trees were passing on either side, far too fast, running away from me until they merged around corners or over hills. The sun was now all but gone, and the trees were only shadow shapes, a great branching mass, split by the stretching, gravel road. The evening was warm and clinging, the speed of the truck the only breeze, drying the sweat on my face.

Gravel ground loudly beneath the tires, rolling and skidding, as the truck braked beside a driveway. Faces emerged beyond the rail.

"Shit, Denis, could you stop any louder?" someone whispered. "My parents think we're sleeping out at the barn."

"Aren't you a bit old for sneaking around on your parents, Adam? You're in college, man."

"Shut up, Denis. You're scared of my mom too." Everyone laughed.

A set of lanky limbs climbed over the side of the truck and settled against the cab beside me. Another set followed it, sat on the wheel well, then reached back to help up a smaller figure, slimmer, with hair like a swaying shadow.

Adam rapped on the window, waited, rapped again. The window opened. "Let's go," he whispered.

"What's your hurry?"

"Nothing. We just don't feel like waiting around while you two grope each other."

The truck staggered into motion, and for a minute there was only the sound of wheels on gravel.

"Whose the new guy?" Adam asked. He looked at me, met my eyes.

"My nephew."

"You have a nephew? How old is he?"

"I don't know. Hey, kid. How old are you?"

"Twelve."

"Shit! Denis, you brought along a twelve year old? What are you thinking?"

"Easy. He's big for his age. He'll be fine. And it's not like I had a choice. My sister dumped him on me for the weekend."

Adam looked at me again. "I guess." He paused. "Hell! The MacInnis girls are coming. He might even get lucky."

Denis laughed. The truck swerved left, skated on the gravel, then caught purchase again.

"Do you guys have any booze up there? All ours is at Mike's."

"Sure."

I was looking out the back of the truck again, away from Adam and from the couple cuddling on the wheel well. A paper bag crackled, then there was the sound of a bottle being opened. Adam drank, then offered me the bottle. It shone golden in the dim light.

"Drink up, kid. You get to be a big boy tonight."

I tried to look practised as I took the bottle. It was cool in my hands, whiskey by the smell. I turned away and took as long a pull as I could manage, making sure not to choke. I wiped my lips with the back of my hand, still not looking at Adam, leaned forward onto my toes, offered the bottle to the couple. Adam chuckled as I sat back and turned to look at the trees, still passing far too fast, ragged shadows in the darkness.

The trucked stopped again. An old farmhouse stood beside the dark shapes of two barns. It was white and wood-sided, ghostly in the night. Six or eight shadows were sitting on the rail fence, like misshapen crows. They jumped into the grass at our approach, shouting and laughing, their shadow bodies merging and parting as they scrambled up to the road, over the side of the truck, into the bed.

It was crowded now. A girl sat on the near wheel well, almost against my feet, her back to me, closing me off from the group. Somebody stumbled over the tents and sleeping bags and cases of beer that had been set in the middle of the truck, half-fell against the cab between Adam and me, and something cold and metallic brushed my cheek. I flinched back, saw that it was a rifle barrel. Its owner was laughing and cursing. Alcohol hung on his breath.

"Denis!" he yelled through the rear-window. "Stop on the hill by the Burrows' place!"

"Jason, stop yelling in my ear, you idiot."

"I said," Jason's repeated, his voice now a hoarse stage whisper, "stop on the hill by the Burrows' place!" He started giggling.

"Why?"

"Just do it. I'm gonna put on a show."

"Whatever. Just don't take too long."

The truck jumped forward again, then shook as Denis tried to get it into gear. Jason almost fell again, still laughing to himself.

The others in the truck were talking loudly about things meaningful only to themselves: a local girl's supposed pregnancy, the chances of an older brother making the NHL, a litany of drunken exploits. The bottle was passed from hand to hand, but it was never passed to me again.

Jason's rifle was standing on its butt end, cradled in his arm. It pressed against my shoulder whenever he leaned forward to see around the girl in front of me or to take the bottle from her. I kept my face away from him, peering over the edge of the truck to where the streaks of gravel whiteness blurred past. I looked up now and again to the shape of the girl on the wheel well, only just female in the dark. She had blonde hair, I thought, but it could have been dark. There was not enough light even to tell that much. Her voice was deep for a girl, like a smoker's.

The truck slowed, less suddenly than before, as if Denis was uncertain where to stop. Jason leapt to his feet and looked out over the cab. "A bit further," he called. The truck edged forward. "Good, good." He hefted the rifle, loaded it on top of the cab, looked down the sight.

"What are you doing up there?" Denis asked.

Jason whooped loudly, like a Hollywood Indian. "Everybody up. Have a look."

I was close by, just at his left elbow. The headlights of the truck were shining down a slight hill. There was a tee intersection at the bottom with a stop sign reflecting the glare back redly. The sound of the first shot startled me. I flinched back, almost falling from the truck, and someone laughed behind me. Jason didn't seem to notice. He sighted and fired again. This time there was a pinging sound from the bottom of the hill, and the sign rocked slightly in the harsh light.

"Whoo!" Jason shouted, looking back to his audience, his eyes shining in his pale face. "One for two, baby!"

"How long is this gonna take?" someone asked.

"I got ten shots, and I'm gonna use them." He fired rapidly now, hardly moving between shots. The sign vibrated almost continually to the sound of pinging bullets. Jason counted as he shot: ping, "Two for three," ping, "Three for four," ping, "Four for five." He counted his ten, never missed again. "Nine for ten!" he crowed, holding his gun aloft like a terrorist on television.

"And them stop signs is quick," someone drawled. Everyone laughed.

"Shut up!" Jason called back. "You couldn't do better."

"I don't go shootin' signs much," the voice replied. "They makes tough eatin'." There was laughter again.

"Hey! Can I go now?" Denis demanded.

"Sure, man, sure." Jason patted the top of the cab.

The truck ground into gear again before most people could find their seats. I sat where I was standing, but there were screams and then more laughter as one of the girls half-fell from the truck and had to be helped back in.

The road after the tee became a track, two gravel ruts with weeds growing up between them and on both sides. The trees were close enough that they reached out over us, sometimes meeting in a canopy, shutting out even the little moonlight that managed to pierce the clouds. The headlights reflected from the trees strangely, lighting the way up like a tunnel, a cone of light through a long cylinder of darkness. The branches seemed like arms threatening to tear us away.

The truck was quieter now. Jason had drunk himself almost to sleep, and the couples were more interested in each other than in conversation. The girl at the wheel well leaned on the edge of the truck and looked back. "Jason, are you drunk already?"

"Shut up," he mumbled. He didn't bother to open his eyes.

The girl met my gaze, as if by mistake. I didn't look away, so she did. The reflections along the tunnel of trees showed her hair was blond, like I thought. Her face was broad, manly, with a strong jaw and a heavy brow. She turned back to me after a moment, embarrassed by the silence. "I'm Liz," she said, "Liz MacInnis."

"Hi," I said.

There was another embarrassed moment. "Who are you?"

"Denis' nephew."

"Oh." She squinted. "Do you have a name?"

I shrugged. "Yep."

She looked offended. "Fine," she said, and turned her back to me again.

The blurring of the trees and the gravel slowed, then everything tilted steeply as we began to climb the first of the dunes. The tunnel of trees was replaced by dark mounds of sand and by the darker hollows between them. Plants grew along the tops of the dunes like bristles on the backs of sleeping animals, silhouetted by the lights of the truck. There were already a few campfires, the glow lighting up the dunes right to their crests, like little suns behind sand horizons. There were other trucks parked here and there, wherever there was a spot. Tents were pitched beside them, dark domes, like sand dunes in miniature.

People began climbing out of the truck even before it stopped. Only Adam stayed, sleeping soundly now. I waited too, until everything had been unloaded. I could hear the sounds of bottles being opened and tents being raised in the darkness. The moon emerged from behind the thinning clouds. I slumped down against the cab and set my feet on the wheel well, looked up into the night to watch the its coming and going.

"Hey!" I heard Denis call. He was leaning over the side of the truck. "I threw your sleeping bag in the tent. Adam's sleeping in his brother's tent, so it's just you and me." His teeth flashed white. "And Jenn."

"Did you put my duffle bag in there too?"

"What duffle bag?"

"The blue one? With my clothes and swim suit and everything?"

"Oh shit, man! I thought that was your gym bag. I left it in the garage when I cleaned out the truck today."

I sat up. "You what?"

"Sorry, kid. I didn't know."

"So what am I gonna sleep in?"

He shrugged. "Just sleep in what you're wearing. It's only one night."

"And what about swimming?"

"Nobody's going swimming, kid. They're just gonna hang out, and drink a bit, and talk shit." He tipped a half-full beer bottle to his lips and finished it with one long pull.

"So what am I supposed to do?"

He tossed the bottle into the darkness. "Just relax. Find a girl to talk to. Go get yourself a beer. Just don't tell your mother I let you. And don't go puking all over yourself. I still have to drive you home in the morning."

He turned away. Someone turned on a radio. The music was cut loudly with static. I laid back again, tried to glimpse the moon, but it was a long time coming. I gave it up and swung myself over the side of the truck.

I walked away from the campfires, down along the beach. The moon came out again, longer now. It struck the peaks of the waves, flickering, like the firelight on the peaks of the dunes. I was between them, the fire and the moon. I took off my sandals and carried them. My feet made long, dragging prints in the cool sand, a broken line between the waves and the dunes, away from the radio and the laughter and the firelight. The dry sand at the surface shifted under my feet, exposed the damp sand beneath, smelling of wetness.

The sand at last gave way to alvar, and I stopped at the edge of the rock, not wanting to risk my feet on the stones in the dark. The beach curved past me, and the headland made a silhouette, blurred against the night. I looked for the exact place where the trees gave way to sky, but it eluded me. The breeze off the water was gentle and cool. The waves only licked at the shore.

I turned back, retracing my path, felt its marks with my feet. The light of the nearest campfire was visible over the dunes. I looked steadily at it, would have missed the three figures sitting against the last of the dunes, but I heard one of them say, half-whispered, "Hey, look. That's the kid. Denis' nephew." I recognized Liz' voice, deep and masculine. "The no-name kid?" one of the others asked, whispering too, then louder, "Hey kid! They don't have names where you come from?" They three of them laughed.

I walked past them toward the campfire. There were four tents around it, one of them ours. Denis and Jenn were half-sitting in front of it, not far from the fire. They had a sleeping bag pulled up over them. Denis was kissing Jenn's neck, and they were laughing about something.

"Hey," I said, and Denis looked up.

"Are you having fun yet, kid?" He tried to sound teasing, but he looked annoyed. He leaned back on one arm, disentangling himself from Jenn's body. The sleeping bag fell open a little, and I saw she had only her underwear on now.

"I want to go swimming."

"I told you, nobody's going swimming!" he said. His voice was exasperated, no longer teasing.

"Yeah, well, then I'll go by myself. Do you have some shorts I can borrow?"

"Listen, kid." He was trying to keep his temper in front of his friends, but his rising volume betrayed his frustration. "The water will be freezing, okay? And you shouldn't swim by yourself anyway. Your mother will kill me if you drown."

"I'm not going to drown," I said, my voice raised a little too. "So do you have shorts I can borrow or not?" The others around the campfire were quiet.

Denis sat up in the sleeping bag, his eyes angry. "Don't give me any shit, kid! I said you're not swimming, so you're not swimming! Got it?"

Everyone's eyes were on me now, like they expected me to do something, throw a punch maybe, or start crying. Denis looked past me, noticed his friends watching. His expression became uncomfortable.

"I am going swimming," I said, and I started taking off my clothes. I didn't turn around to see if people were watching, and I didn't look at Denis either, just at Jenn, like she was the only one there. I made myself do it slowly, so I wouldn't seem embarrassed. I folded everything carefully and piled it on my sandals.

"Well," Jenn said softly, "he's not shy, is he?" There was whispering behind me, but no one else said anything out loud. Then, as causally as I could, like I did it all the time, I walked naked between the dunes, toward the water.

# The Edge Of Everything

I have a memory of a somewhere I cannot now find, a wooden pier and a broad bay and a rocky shore, a somewhere that I will never recognize again, because I was so young, and because my memories of that day are vast and ambiguous, the kind of memories that I have onlyfrom my early childhood, though I was already old enough then to be helping my younger brother detangle his fishing line, knotted in great loops of slender nylon. The lake was immense, massive under a massive sky, and I was small, dangling my line and myself over the edge of a broad expanse, over a bit of dock that jutted only a short way past the edge of everything. I don't grow memories like that anymore, and I have a longing for them, for that world, broad and undefined, a world more of potential than of actuality.

In that world, as I worked to straighten my brother's

line, a fish rose to the surface, or what counted as a fish to us anyway, a sunfish probably, or maybe a rock bass, a perch at best, hardly worth keeping, certainly not worth the agony that it was about to cause. Only my brother saw it rise and nibble at the tain of the water, but in my mind, like so many other fish I've seen, it eases slowly up from the piling of the dock, waits inches below the surface, its body half turned, strikes on whatever bit of drifting food has drawn it from hiding, and then I can see my brother's rod thrusting at the water and the line growing taut in my hand, but mostly I can feel the hook drawing up into my thumb, the line tugging at my flesh.

My grandfather cut the line fast enough, I'm sure, and I'm also sure that my young imagination exaggerated the pain beyond all proportion, but even now that hook hurts me more than any other injury I've ever suffered. I screamed, and I kept screaming, my grandfather, with his unrelenting patience, saying all the while that screaming wasn't helping anything, that closing my eyes would make it hurt less, and then he took advantage of my blindness to grab the hook with the pliers and push the barb through the heel of my thumb in one swift pain. I opened my eyes in time to see him snip the barb and pull the hook back through the wound. I laid on the dock, rough and wooden, my head turned to one side to feel the weather-etched grain against my cheek as he bandaged my thumb, with what I can't remember, a ripped shirt maybe, or a rag from the car.

# Of These True Things

Of these true things God made the North:
Of rock and water, trees and sky;
All else comes falsely, even earth,
And like the earth we thinly lie
Upon its face, constrained by birth
To cling in wonder til we die.

# Across The Lake

The morning is not yet light, only luminous, only lapping at the edge of light with the crests of its shallow waves and its whisping clouds, but the docks are not empty, not even so early. There are boats setting out into the bay, their prows cutting scallops of foam to swell into the dawn, and there is the bobbing head of a swimmer too, white-capped, rising and falling, like a bit of foam itself, moving against the water toward the piers of the old wharf, most of which has long since fallen away, leaving only islands of cement to mark the point around which boats must come to negotiate the harbour and on which the gulls gather in their hundreds to gossip and strut and wait for the next fishing boat to breast the point.

The gravel crunches hollowly beneath my feet along the shoulder of a road that was once asphalt but is now dissolving into its component parts, becoming indistinguishable from the hollowly crunching gravel of the shoulder. There are apple trees along the road, the fruit not yet ripe, feral, never thinned, hanging too heavily on the branches. The trees line both sides of the road and press up against the few houses of the village. I thin the fruit absently while I walk, as I do every time I trace the shoulder of the road between the apple trees, solitary, lingering above the quiet foam of the harbour waves. The unripe apples go skipping, hard and green, in among the trunks, my targets chosen at random, as often missed as hit.

I turn from the gravel, looking back one last time at the water through the apple trees, brighter now already, the sun glancing off the waves, blurring the boats and their foam scallops, the bobbing white cap on its way to the piers. The ground underfoot is now sod, brown so late in the summer, and sandy, as if the heat of the past few weeks has drawn the sand up from the soil as it has drawn the moisture up from the grass.

There are the remains, also, of a long ago garden, potentilla bushes shot full of yellow flowers, ladyslippers pink and yellow, raspberries just in full fruit, choke cherries hanging heavy but still unripe, wild roses, bearberry, anemone, bluet, lobelia. They are struggling too, against the encroaching grasses and the weeds, struggling, like the crumbling piers, straining to keep their heads above the water, like a blurred speck of white-capped head, bobbing against the waves.

# Orchard Fence

There was a thick swath of grass along the fenceline, growing up around the old unpruned rosebushes, their hollow stems become highways for ants. The riding-mower was too clumsy, never got close enough, always left this border of dandelions and burdock and flowering thorns, and made a hedge of the fenceline that ran around the old orchard, now the horse paddock, between the house and the barn. We waded that hedge and climbed its fence most days, on both sides of the orchard, to and from milking in the morning, to and from the house at lunch if we were haying, preferring to make our paths through the grasses and leap the fence rather than walk the few yards more around the paddock.

The two horses who inhabited the orchard, any of a long succession of Queens and Macs, usually Belgians, sometimes Percherons, taking their names from their predecessors like batons in a relay, never bothered with us, content to rest their satin bulk wherever the grazing was best. When we paused to climb the apple trees, though, they knew to follow, their ears pricking hopefully as they circled the trunks and nosed the lower branches, waiting for us to pick the apples that grew too high for them.

We sat in the gnarled branches of the fruit trees, our backs pressed against the bark, feeling the deep grooves of the tree's skin against our own, and we tossed apples to one another through the branches. The light filtered through the green of apple leaves, a warm and golden green, and a red tinged green too, all of it sun-warm and shade-cool beneath the arches of the trees, scented with apples rotting into sweetness at the feet of our perches.

The horses rooted in the grass for the apples we could not catch, hunting as surely as hounds, but placidly, knowing that their prey would not outrun them. When we tired of throwing our misshapen projectiles, we lured them to us with proffered fruit, and they consented to be led beneath us, though they surely knew by then that we would leap astride them, bareback, less riding them than lying precariously atop their broad strength, allowing ourselves to be carried by them, by their animal redolence and by the sun-warmth of their skin, until we lost our grasp and fell, fearfully, gloriously, into the tall grass along the fence.

# This String Of Eyeless Fish

My cousin's grandfather has cut our holes for us with the auger, and we have dropped our lines, just lengths of twine with hooks, baited with worms at first and then the eyes of the fish we have caught, the dead going to catch the living. We have no way to reel in our lines when we feel a bite, so we run with them across the ice until the the fish come flopping behind us in the snow. This is what I remember, the running, never waiting, only running, as if we did nothing but drag perch from the lake all that night. There's a picture of us still, in an album of my mother's, or maybe my father's, all of us standing with our catch on a string, all of us who were big enough to go fishing at the time, three or four of us anyway, all wrapped in our winter gear and smiling past this string of eyeless fish.

# Beneath The Norisle

The switchback from the town to the docks turns sharply downward toward the old mill, then back past the theatre on our left, and finally out toward the beach. We leave our things up under the pavilion and then go straight to fishing from the long docks. The boys who are hired to run the marine fuelling station watch us with amusement, knowing as well as we do that there is little or nothing to be caught. We watch them too, their feet up on the windows of the booth, talking, smoking, tossing stones into the water, and infrequently, filling up a boat that is either lost enough to find its way into the harbour at Manitowaning or bored enough to visit the rusting hulk of the Norisle.

I leave the others to fish, walk up along the side of the retired ferry, the sun-hot gravel giving way to the shadow-cool grass in the shelter of the boat's bulk. There is a cormorant atop its radio tower, and it leaves its shadow too, indistinct so far below, but visible if you know to look for it.

Further along the shore the sun returns, and the beach is rocky, bending away behind the mill. I follow the threshold of land and water to where the vegetation begins to grow up along it, where the reeds and the shrubs obscure it, and see a small school of brown trout, lingering along the line of rock where the lake floor drops suddenly deeper. The day is clear, and the lake is still, and I can see a long way beneath the water, see the four of them marking the place where the pale and shallow green descends into a deeper blue. Three of them are a true brownish colour, the other one more silver, their dark spots showing sharply in the clearness of the water, the sun illuminating their fins like broken halos. They move slowly, hardly seeming to move, drifting in tandem with their shadows, a double school of fish, until they find the shelter of the ship, become one with their shadows, and their halos are extinguished. They hover there a long while, and I think about getting my rod from the dock, but it is more pleasure to watch them than to catch them, so I let them be until they turn together and head away under the ferry out into the lake.

# Snapper

There is a turtle in the hoopnet, I can see right away, a snapper, almost always, lured by the fish through the narrowing hoops, one after the other, its claws now gripping the netting. We aren't supposed to kill them, and prying them out of the net is impossible, so we will have to cut the net, take the turtle out, mend the hole before resetting the trap. My uncle would have been impatient, but he isn't with us today, just my grandfather and I, pulling the nets for pike.

We lift the front end first, funnelling any straggling fish through the hoops, deeper into the net, but I don't see any fish yet, just the broad round hoops bound one to the other by a sheath of netting, like old-fashioned dresses sewn in a line, or like a sea-serpent with its ribs showing. The netting is covered with silt and algae, tangled with waterweeds, slippery and cumbersome and heavy with wet. The smell is of fish and shallow waters and mud and rot, but somehow wholesome, the sort of smell that promises growing things, not cultivated, but fecund and burgeoning and profligate. It settles over the boat, tangibly fertile, as if shoots might sprout from it in the warmth of the sun, cover the boat with vegetation, make an island of it in the shallow bay.

The last hoop, square, larger than the others, lies just below the surface, the turtle clinging to the top of it, and below, in the mote-filled water, the fish hover, slim, quavering, mottled. Their broad tails are like fletching on loosed and darting arrows, and they are most beautiful now, in mid flight, before they are surfaced, to lie flapping and breathless.

The nets lift from the water, suddenly lighter, and fall into the boat. I untie the closure, dump the fish onto the deck, no longer quavering, just slithering. There are only three, and the snapper has been at the smallest of them, almost severing its head and eating away most of its belly. The larger two, still struggling, are tossed into the totes.

I take my knife and cut the net around the snapper's claws, pull the turtle, with the patch of net it has claimed, from the hoop and toss it into the prow. It's no good putting it back into the water here to catch again next time, so we'll take it with us when we leave, drop it far from the nets somewhere. It's a male, I think, because the tail is so wide, but it's harder to tell with snappers. Their tails are longer than other turtles, tougher to gauge. He pulls himself along the deck, his claws rasping the metal, his shell knocking the sides of the boat.

My grandfather is looking at the hole I have made in the net, seeing if it can be repaired now or if it will need to come back with us. He has tipped his hat back on his head to see better, the rounded brim tilted skyward, the mesh back almost slipping off the baldness of his head. He pulls from his pocket a yellow plastic mending needle, the same colour as his slicker, threads it with twine, and makes the attempt, though the hole looks large. This might take him some time, and we are drifting toward the shore, in among the reeds, so I toss out the anchor, watching it descend out of sight into the shallow murk.

I sit myself on the tote, put my feet up on the spare nets, then remember my coffee set beside the helm, but I decide to leave it, pulling my cap down over my eyes against the water's glare. I am well enough awake by now, and warm too, though it was cold this morning when we untied from the jetty, early enough that the sun was only an orange dye tinging the black-blue of the water. It had been calm this morning too, the water barely stirring the dock, twisting it gently with the irregular rhythm that only waves can keep, and the thermos had been hot in my hand, while the rest of me was morning-cold, waking-cold, waiting bodily for the sun to warm the world beyond the power of the thin cool breezes.

It is well warm now though, my hat ringed with sweat

around the brim, and the corners of my mouth tasting
salt, and it is bright, the sun striking obliquely on the
faces of the low swells, on the aluminium of the boat,
on the whiteness of the rocks. It is a brightness that
comes from everywhere, that leaves no true shadow, only
infinite numbers of tenuous, quivering shadows, like the
spots on the sides of pike as they hover, refracted, just
beneath the membrane of the water, like schools of min-
nows swarming the shallows with their shadow doubles,
like whirligig beetles running the stillness of the water to
riot.

The snapper is in the front of the boat, trying to climb
the aluminium sides, but the metal is too slick, and its
legs are too short to reach even the tie bar, never mind the
gunwale, so its claws rasp futilely, merely polishing the
metal to shine more brightly in the sun, to cast brighter
gleams, to make more vibrating shadow. It never pauses
in its labour though, scratching a steady counter rhythm
to the irregular slapping of waves on the hull and to the
gurgling wash of still other waves against the shore.

The shore is rocky here, long and rock strewn, flooded
in spring but dry now. The trees, back a hundred yards
or so from the water, are stunted and tortured, as though
they now regret having put down roots here, clutching at
the rock through the thin soil just to survive the winter
storms and the spring floods and the summer droughts.
Their lower branches are all dead. It is only their upper-
most limbs that have any life in them, springing green

and surprising from the desolation below them.

We stopped to eat here once, making a fire from the dead wood in among the dry, pebbling stones further up the beach, where the trees begin, gutting the unsaleable fish, the carp and the catfish and the suckers, then frying them quickly in butter, our only condiment. They taste good, the garbage fish, as long as they are eaten like this, immediately after they are killed, before they have time to grow fishy, even better if I can find wild leeks around, as I sometimes can.

We threw the guts in the lake, and the crayfish were soon clambering over them. I sat on a shelf of rock to watch the lake as the fish cooked, smelling the woodsmoke and the butter, and then I saw a northern water snake come out from under the rocks away to my left, nosing about for the fish guts too. Most snakes won't eat carrion, but northern water snakes will, or they'll eat dead fish anyway, and they'll sometimes eat their food tail first too, which I've never seen another snake do. The bands on this one were still very red, though it was an adult length, red and deep brown, alternating, like a row of saddles for miniature riders. It reared its head a little and circled past the discarded fish, then slipped wholly into the water, making the water ripple convulsively as it gulped its meal, little splashes disturbing the pattern of the lapping waves.

The snapper's churning claws return me to the boat. My grandfather is bent patiently over the net. He has cut a patch from a piece of spare netting kept for just this purpose, and he is sewing it in place, firmly, methodically, which is his way. There is never any fuss about him, never any hurry. Now and again he wipes the perspiration from his head with the sleeve of his plaid cotton shirt, but he never looks up, sewing steadily in big looping stitches, until he is tying the line off, testing it, holding it up for my inspection.

"Let's get this set then," he says as he stands, and I am about to stand as well, when I hear the sound of the snapper's claws suddenly stop.

Standing in the front of the boat, the turtle is stretching its neck toward the tie bar, stretching to a remarkable length, looking more like a snake slipping out of a crevice than a turtle at all. It closes its jaws around the bar and begins to pull itself upward, incrementally, by the strength of its neck alone, drawing its body after it, dangling by its jaws. Its feet hover above the deck until its shell is almost level with is beak, high enough that it can reach the tie bar with its claws. Then, with remarkable ease, even grace, it pulls itself the last few inches over the rail and slaps into the water, disappears into the reeds and mud.

# Into The Shallows

We are sitting, all of us boys, some cousins too, in the mouth of the river at Providence Bay, and it is evening, late in the year, one of the last times we will swim that season, and the water is warm beneath the cool of the air. I am half-sitting, my legs folded under me, pulling the water back and forth with my arms, and then I feel something in my lap, a bunch of water weeds perhaps, so I reach down, and I find in my hands a salmon, almost still, alive but apparently unafraid. I take my hands away in reflex, but when I return them the salmon is there still, and so, as much by reflex again as by thought, I stand, lift it from the water, and toss it onto the bank.

It lies in the sand, its colour muted in the dusk, flapping lethargically. Wading out of the water, I kneel beside it, lay my hand on its side, but I cannot bring myself to return it to the water somehow, not until a passerby

103

begins yelling about how fishing is illegal there. So I lift it again, cradle it more like, walk it back into the shallows, release it, my body cold and shivering, but I want it back again the next moment, not just any fish, but that fish, the one I have been holding, because it is more real to me now than all the others, singular and irreplaceable.

# Shallow Earth

Where the loggers have levelled the ground along the access road, the earth, shallow, has been scraped away, revealing layers of sand and, in places, finally, the stratified rock of the shield. Trees dangle along these wounds, their roots trailing into the void, suspended in space, holding tenuous clutches of topsoil in their many-toed feet, holding clumps of moist darkness that appear to hover above the lightness of the sand and the rock. The sand has sometimes eroded so far that appearance has become reality, hollows forming beneath the fabric of roots and earth and moss, leaving the trees floating above the insubstantial air, their weight twisting, then finally breaking the carpet of vegetation, leaning, falling into the level, barren spaces that the loggers have abandoned.

# Earthen Skies

I lay where the summer had surprised me,
beneath a tree, half lightning blasted, limbs
like roots burrowing into a thin, blue,
transparent soil, the trunk suspended there
above a green, impenetrable sky,
adrift between two heavens and two earths,
surrounded by long shadows, sun flung
and invisible, branches become roots
then cast, insubstantial, on earthen skies.

# Dappled

There are moments for which adequate words do not come to us until the moments themselves have long turned to memories, until we stumble on words that did not seem possible to us, words that come upon us unaware and return our moments to us transfigured, as when I first came upon a poem of dappled things, of things counter, original, spare, strange, fickle, freckled, swift, slow, sweet, sour, adazzle, dim, and I saw again a river that I had once known, a river with skies as couple-coloured as a brinded cow, with trout stippled in rose-moles, with finches wings, dappled, a dappled river, because though we never caught any of the rose-stippled trout, ever, we caught cool mornings with breezes that ran up along the stream bed, and we caught afternoons too hot to move except if we were knee deep in the water with the silver maples casting their shadows overhead and with the light broken by the

113

leaves and then broken again by the ripples of the water, dappled like that, and that's why we kept fishing there, because the river was too perfect not to fish, too shaded and clear and overhung by banks of weeds and branches, too meandering and full of still pools and sudden holes, too dappled.

# The Diner

The diner is just across the border of the reserve, filled about equally with local residents and with the cottagers who lease property from the band. The laws against smoking in public places don't apply here, and many of the cottagers come here just for that reason, so the dining room is filled with smoke.

There are three officers from the reserve police in the corner closest to the kitchen, farthest from my own table. They speak to the cook through the open doorway with the ease of regulars. They are tall and well-built, all of them, with closely cut dark hair and handsome faces, wearing very clean, very sharp uniforms, complete with bullet-proof vests and hand guns and brushed caps set carefully on the table beside their plates. They know they are the symbols of a new kind of reserve that takes care of its own business. Much of the reserve is lagging behind them, of course, but they are a symbol of what is possible, law and order and beautiful uniforms, all with a native face.

They are drinking coffee from white diner mugs, and one calls into the kitchen, "Hey, Susan, has that Barbeau kid come around since we picked him up?"

"Nope. Haven't seen him," a woman's voice replies, disembodied, emerging from the kitchen, throaty and sensual, a smoker's voice. "You guys didn't rough him up too badly did you? He's really not a bad kid."

"He took cash from you at knife point, Susan. He's a bad kid."

"He just steals because his mother steals."

"Maybe, but she steals for booze. He just does it for kicks. He's gonna be a mean one when he gets older."

"The band should have done something earlier, placed him with an auntie."

"That's what they'd do now, for sure." He sipped from his mug. "But times were different then."

"Says the boy talking to his grandma."

The three officers all laugh, bright and handsome.

The girl in the next booth looks up at them and then away again before they can meet her eyes. She is sipping from a mug of coffee also, staring across at an elderly woman in a pink, floral hat, humped over a pot of tea. The girl is thin, not like an anorexic or an athlete, but like someone whose body only ever bothered to grow upward, spent all its energy on height and had nothing left over for roundness, for breasts or hips. Her eyes look past the old woman without interest, past the pink hat with its white and blue flowers, past the hand-knitted pink shawl and the blue dress with its delicately scalloped collar. She looks at the same time fierce and bored.

"How's your soda, Lamby?" the old woman asks.

The girl's eyes focus for an instant on the elderly face and then drift into the distance again. "It's not soda Grandma. It's coffee. And nobody calls it soda anymore. It's called pop." She fidgets, running her thumb along the inside of her necklace, rearranging the salt and pepper shakers, spinning her rings on her fingers. Her eyes drift across the restaurant towards my table. I look down to my breakfast until her gaze passes over me, just another teen boy eating his breakfast.

The older woman seems either not to hear or not to care. She sips daintily from her teacup, the perfect caricature of a grandmother.

"Will you need me this afternoon, Grandma?" the girl asks. Her mouth hardly ever moves, even when she speaks.

"What's that?" The older woman tilts her head to the left and leans toward her granddaughter.

"I said, do you need me for anything this afternoon?"

"No, not today, Lamby. I think I'll have a bit of a nap after lunch. You go ahead and have the afternoon to yourself."

The girl takes a cigarette from her purse and puts it between her lips but leaves it unlit. "Can I have the car?" she says. The cigarette twitches in time to her words.

"You know I never let anyone drive it without me," her grandmother replies, "and you know I can't abide smoking, so put that dirty thing away."

"It's not lit, Grandma." She takes the cigarette from her mouth, turns it between her fingers until it breaks, tosses it into the ashtray. "Please, Grandma. Daniel's parents won't let him use the car anymore. And he says he shouldn't come into town for a while. Can't I take it just this once?"

"I certainly will not send you off unattended with my car to see some, some Indian. Certainly not."

"Native, Grandma. He's native. It's rude to say Indian."

"I don't care what you call him. You may not take my car."

The girl stands up and grabs her bag from the seat. "Fine," she says, "I'm going for a smoke," and she stalks to the door, her heels clicking hollowly on the linoleum floor.

"You're allowed to smoke in here, you know," says a man as she passes his table. She ignores him and pushes her way out through the door. He shrugs and leans on the table, its edge pressing deeply into the heavy flesh of his bare forearms.

"Did you see that?" he demands. The woman across from him never bothers to look up, keeps her eyes on the newspaper, almost tenderly tapping the ash of her cigarette into the ashtray. Her silence doesn't deter him. He lights a cigarette of his own. "So rude," he says, brushing his long hair out of his face, his eyes squinting in the smoke as he exhales. "First we almost hit that one kid. Runs into the road right in front of us. Gives me the finger when I slam on the breaks, like I didn't just save his life."

He leans back in his chair, pulls his t-shirt down over his belly. "Then that skinny chick..." he stops himself and looks at the old lady across the restaurant. "Then that skinny chick, " he continues, his voice lower, "gives me a look like that. For trying to be nice." He shakes his head and idly moves his homefries around his plate. "Are you listening to me, Jessica?"

The woman makes no sign that she has heard him. Her blond hair hangs long on either side of her face. It swings slightly as her eyes follow the print in front of her.

"Hey!" the man says suddenly, and something in his voice seems to register with Jessica enough for her to look up as well. "It's that kid!" he hisses, half-whispering. "The kid we almost hit!"

Jessica turns in her chair, looks behind me to the back door, and I turn too. A boy, a bit older than me, stands just inside the door, peering around the angle of the hallway into the restaurant. The couple by the door can see him, and so can I, but the wall hides him from everyone else. He seems intent on the booth where the girl had been sitting, then he notices the three officers and presses further back into the door jamb. His dark hair is long and pulled into a ponytail.

The front door opens, and the girl walks in, her jeans hanging low on her thin hips. She looks to her left, past the couple by the door, past my table, to the boy hiding in the back hall. Her eyes widen, and she smiles shyly, checks to see whether her grandmother is watching. "Um, Grandma," she calls, "I'm just going to the bathroom, okay?"

Her grandmother looks over the top of her glasses. "Sure, Lamby."

The girl crosses the diner to the hallway and throws her arms around the boy's neck, her shirt pulling up to show a bird tattoo in the small of her back. She tries to kiss his face, but he looks distracted, whispers something in her ear. She looks over her shoulder to where the three officers are leaning back in their chairs, coffees in hand. He tries to lead her outside, but she opens the door to the bathroom and pulls him in. There is lettering on the back of his leather jacket. "Grizzlies," it reads, over a logo of a bear, and then underneath, "Daniel Barbeau, Left Wing."

"I should've known," says the man by the door. He scratches the stubble on his face. "Those two were meant for each other." Jessica has already gone back to her paper.

I finish my food, but the waitress hasn't been by in a long while. I think about going to ask for my bill, but the reserve police get up first. "Bill please, Susan," one calls.

"Separate?" comes the throaty voice.

"Naw, put it all together. And put my coffee tab on there too."

"Sure."

"Thanks, Eric. I'll get it next time," one of the others says. "I'm just gonna use the can." He leaves his hat on the table and strolls across the restaurant to the bathroom, tries the handle. There's no sound from inside. "Hey," he asks, "is someone in there?" There's still silence. He tries the door again. "Susan?" he calls, "I think someone locked the bathroom on you."

"It's just a toothpick lock," she shouts back. "Go ahead and open it."

The officer knocks again. "I'm coming in, " he says, "so speak up if you're in there." The sudden sound of glass smashing comes from inside the bathroom, like a window has been broken out, and then a scrambling noise. "What the hell?" the officer says. He doesn't bother finding a toothpick, just steps back and breaks the door in with a kick. It swings open on its hinges and bangs against the inside of the wall. A girl's voice starts screaming, and I can see the skinny girl pressed into the far corner of the bathroom, her face in her hands. The officer leaps to stand on the rim of the toilet, peering out through the broken window on the opposite wall. "It's no use running, Barbeau," he yells. "You've got no where to go!"

He comes back into the restaurant. One of the other officers throws him his cap, and all three dash through the door.

"Be gentle with him!" Susan yells after them, then quieter, so only we can hear, "He's really not a bad kid."

# A Slender Pine

There is, through the window, a slender pine,
A shadow shape against a shadowed night,
A charcoal wick aflame with a hazed moon,
Pallid, flickering, and all adrift
Of the world, astride the pine's upstretched peak,
The silhouetted ache of earth for sky.

# When It Was Theirs

I am standing in the room that was built to be theirs, added as an inner sanctum to what is otherwise only a hunting camp in the bush. The rest of the cabin is a single room, cedar posts sealed with mortar outside and nothing at all inside, heated by a woodstove, furnished with timber bunkbeds, roofed in tin. This added room, though, it is sided in split cedar outside and panelled with cut cedar inside, a small room that once had its own wood stove also, when it was theirs, and it had certainly been warm then, though it is cold now.

There are boxes of their things stacked under the window, the bits of their life that were too insignificant to be be moved to the new cabin, the one insulated and plumbed and wired, almost a house. I leave everything where it is, but I can see some of her spy novels in the tops of the boxes, a framed map of the waters around the island, a picture of their youngest son at the wheel of a fishing boat, an orange safety vest, a piece of wood with a Bible verse painted on it. There is a cake of green rat poison sitting on top of it all, and there is another in the far corner, a third on the bedside table. The bed is stripped to the mattress, leaving only coverless pillows, and everything is sprinkled with a fine dusting of pine needles.

In one corner, beside a cake of poison, there are marks on the floor where the woodstove once was. A hole gapes above it, like a wound that has released the soul of the place, leaving only this behind: the boxes of unwanted things, the nameless green poison, the uncovered bed, the litter of needles.

# The Gulls

The ragged clouds of gulls pass overhead,
frayed and straggling, black against a grey sky,
chasing the last fragments of the sun,
each tethered to the next by stray wings,
in twos or threes, clutches, sprays of shadow
that spring from occluding forest
to be swallowed by indefinite horizon,
like bits of ash returning to the fire that first flung them
into the high and cooling air of a still un-starred sky.

# In Sprays Of Silver

I was idly casting from the dock, just to be alone and to be on the dock and not to be playing cards in the cottage kitchen. I was standing on a bit of walkway on the far side of the boathouse, and I don't remember that exact moment very clearly, but I've stood in that same spot many times before and since, so I know that I was listening to the sound of the motorboat nodding against the rubber bumpers, making the water slap and gurgle, and I was smelling the acid of evergreen forest, sharp, cut with the scent of some not too distant campfire, and I was feeling the temperature fall away with the sun behind the trees, and I was casting a small silver spinner out into the lake.

I have since caught any number of sunfish under that dock with my kids, but I had never seen anything caught there yet when I was casting that evening, so I was star-

tled when I felt a strike on the lure, and more startled still
when the fish ran strongly with the line. When it slacked,
I reeled it in as far as I could, and then the fish ran again
against the line, and it jumped. In sprays of silver, it
jumped, as no other fish ever has, and I stopped reeling,
amazed, paused expectantly, hoping it would jump again,
but then I felt it pull sharply, and the line grew suddenly
slack, and I knew that I'd lost it, and the lure too, the
line was so light. Then, as I was reeling the empty line,
the fish jumped again, almost straight out of the water,
less than thirty yards away, a bit to the left of where I'd
seen it jump first, and it was my fish, I'm sure, because I
heard the jingle of the lure as it thrashed its head in the
cool evening air.

# In The Kitchen

My grandmother always cooked breakfast for the whole Island, it seemed, at least in the summertime, not only for my grandfather and for the hired men, but also for the temporary help, and for her three sons, and for their wives, and for her ten or twelve grandchildren, not to mention anyone who might drop by at the breakfast hour, the vet out to help with a breach birth maybe, or someone asking a question of my grandfather the Reeve. There would be porridge for those who wanted it, and eggs, boiled or fried, and preserves from the pantry, and frozen fruit from the freezer, and honey in the comb from who knows where, and homemade bread covered with home-made butter. My grandfather always took boiled eggs, cooked very soft, thirty seconds or so, just enough to warm them. He would crack the eggs into a bowl and spoon them up with fat slices of bread and butter. Then

143

he would pour himself a whole bowl of maple syrup, made right there on the farm, and that would do for another slice. Whatever syrup was left he would drink straight from the bowl.

There were so many at breakfast sometimes that we ate in shifts, some of us up early enough to help with the chores before sitting at the long table stretching across the farm kitchen, while others would trickle down over the next few hours, much to my grandmother's disapproval. She had no patience for laziness, and the idea of sleeping in was offensive to her, but she would feed the late comers anyway, and they would listen to her lectures about sloth with easy tolerance.

I often sat at that table from the moment I came in from chores until lunch was served, reading my book and watching one shift of breakfasters follow another. My grandmother would hardly leave the kitchen that whole time, maybe just to change some laundry or to bring something up from the basement. She made sandwiches to send to the fields, kneaded dough for bread, rolled pie crusts for the freezer, and processed whatever fruit and vegetables we had picked for her from the garden the day before.

Sometimes I found myself pressed into service, shelling peas or chopping rhubarb or hulling strawberries. Those mornings all drift together, the sun coming through the windows at the end of the table as I look up to see the familiar kitchen things, the squirrel-shaped napkin holder made by some long dead relative, the pot holders kept by my grandparents from their days as missionaries in the islands, and the circa fifties vacuum cleaner, oval and green-blue, standing propped by the pantry.

No matter how early my brothers and I would first wake in the morning, come down the slender stairway with its croaking steps, its picture of Christ knocking on the door of our metaphorical hearts, and its own literal door at the bottom, white and wooden and latched with stubborn cast iron, my grandmother would always be up already. She would seat us on the livingroom couch, keeping an eye on the stove all the while, and quiz us with handmade, pale green, fish-shaped flash cards of Bible trivia: the number of books in the New Testament (twenty-seven, at least for us protestants); the number of silver pieces that Judas received to betray Jesus (thirty); the names of the Hebrew boys thrown into the fiery furnace (Shadrach, Meshach, and Abednego, or To-bed-you-go, as we secretly pronounced it), by which we were able to earn our way, if not heavenward, at least through the kitchen and to the barn.

That is how I remember her, presiding over our passages through the kitchen, bribing us with frozen blueberries covered in milk that soon froze also in shades of lilac and lavender, so that we would consent to the huge vitamin pills and fish oil caplets and garlic tablets that were her secret to health and longevity; conscripting us to take up flyswatters against the bluebottles that waited, as we

146

did, to descend on her pastry the moment her back was
turned; directing us to set up for holiday meals so large
that the tables spilled through the kitchen door to the
livingroom next to it; calling us to stand by our chairs,
hands behind our backs, to recite the verses that I can
even now remember.

# Pel Mel

Oh glory of sun-haloed chaff hanging in newly birthed silence, offspring of the bale-elevator's clamor – clig-clig-clig, clig-clig-clig, clang, clig-clig-clig, clig-clig-clig, clang – interminable, and the engine chanting beneath it all, a noise gestated in the warm closeness of the mow, in its uterine murk, growing as the hay bales rise, one atop the other, first this way then that, filling the womb of the mow, distending it, and the noise – clig-clig-clig, clig-clig-clig, clang, clig-clig-clig, clig-clig-clig, clang – concentrated with the chaff and the heat, throwing itself into the mow like seed into a womb, interminable, until the moment, oh glory of sun-haloed chaff hanging in the doorway of the afternoon, when the long labour is ended and silence lies in the mess of its afterbirth. The breeze, so slight, eddies there in the doorway, with the haloes and the silence, where I am standing. It is too

151

weak even to move the dust of the air, only loiters at the threshold, running over the skin of things, delicately, cautiously, intimately, like blind fingers on an unfamiliar face. It is hiding itself between the heat of the mow and the heat of the sun, in the sliver of shadow that the barn is beginning to cast into the yard, where I am hiding too, on the threshold of the mow, my arms raised to rest against the top jamb of the broad door, leaning out into the yard, like the shadows and like the breeze, attendants at the birth of this sudden quiet, this completion, this expectancy, this waiting for what will come to fill the unforeseen emptiness of an afternoon.

The others have already left the mow, down the ladder, through the void we kept in the hay, layer by layer, to the stairs, then through the barn and the empty stalls and the milkhouse, smelling sweetly of the manure freshly scraped into the gutters and the milk souring where it has spilled on the floor, past the ledge where the basin of milk is set, where the cats can sometimes be surprised and captured, though certainly not without gloves and even then not without risk of bloody arms. I can see them, those others, drifting off beyond the corner of the barn to the farmhouse, where lunch will be on the table now, surely, sandwiches of cow's tongue or egg salad between slices of heavily buttered homemade bread, oatmeal cookies with chopped dates and raisins, freshly pressed carrot juice, but I am hungry only for the unexpected emptiness of the day, for what it might bring, for the haloes that the dust motes wrap around themselves, for the tender fingers of the eddying breeze, for the sliver of shadow resting between one heat and another, for the infant silence that sleeps over everything.

The clinging of my shirt becomes suddenly unbearable, the chaff sticking to the wetness. I pull it over my head and fling it into the yard, floating and twisting, like a bird shot on the wing, drifting and fluttering, passing through the shadow to the sun, landing beneath the wheel of the hay waggon, and I will leave it there, as we have left the waggon, to be collected at the leisure of another time, to become the perfect luxury of an all but completed task. I sit on the elevator, unlace my boots, and throw them too, no fluttering or drifting, only heavy, projectile flight, then my balled socks, tumbling. The air hangs cool on my shoulders and feet, trickles with the sweat down my chest. I let the whole world dangle like my feet, the cool, the shadow, the breeze, the quiet, let it all dangle over the edge of the mow, kicking absently with my heels, awaiting whatever it is that will come, compelling the world to wait with me, kick its heels, feel the air hang cool on its shoulders.

At last, how long, the waiting calls me to my feet and down the elevator, quietly at first, to keep the metal panels from popping, the supports from creaking, but the elevator's voice is insistent. It scoops the infant silence from the shadowed ground, lets it howl its first cries, frees me from caution, so I abandon myself to the clat-

ter of its rungs – clang-clong-cleng, clang-clong-cleng –
a ragged and joyous noise that does not end the silence
but erupts from it, makes it audible, spills and runs and
overflows, like abundance and surplus, like teeming and
proliferation, like deluge and cataclysm, like everything
abundant, extravagant, profuse. My feet, bare, slapping,
are a riot and a tumult of expectation, cool at first, down
the rungs, then suddenly hot, where the shadow ends and
the sun rests itself upon the metal: cool-cool-cool, cool-
cool-cool, hot-hot-hot, hot-hot-hot, and then a leap, into
the grass growing long in the lea of the elevator, smelling
of only what it is, grass and summer and the heat of the
sun.

Oh, and then, as glorious as any halo, I run, pel mel
and trip-trip-tripping on chicory and wild carrot and bur-
dock, what the cows will not eat, stumble and tumble on
the hems of my jeans, too long for barefoot and frayed
besides and split at the knees and worn to white thread
at the thighs by bale after bale – hup, up on the thigh,
and toss, and hup, up on the thigh, and toss – but no
more, not for another year, so I tear the jeans at the
knees until the legs dangle by the seams, cut them away
with my knife, cut them like traces from a horse, leave it
all in a pile and run free, bare-kneed now and bare-foot,
like Tom Sawyer and Huck Finn and Johnny Appleseed,
bare-foot in the cow-meadow.

The meadow runs too, slow and liquid, like honey, like
intoxication, like honey-wine, like mead, running, run-

ning, and the bees rise in alarm from their pollen-feasts, fly off to make mead of the meadow. I throw myself into that mellifluence, drink its sweetness up, not merely lapping it from cupped hands like the wise three hundred, nor even drinking it straight from the stream like the foolish thousands, but leaping into its depths, breathing it in, filling my lungs with it, even to drowning. It is equal parts honey and the blood of gods, this meadow wine, a drink that makes wise, but there are no words for this wine's wisdom. Its truths are written in the petals of asters and fleabane and bergamot, held fast to the flesh by sweet-salt sweat, legible only to the meadow, summer-hot, insect-droned, pollen-hazed.

The grasshoppers scatter at my feet, helter-skelter-pelter, then settle to wait and scatter once again – pht-t-t-t-t, pht-t-t-t-t, pht-t-t-t-t – my emissaries, the vanguard of my advance. They make a way for me, put everything in readiness for my coming, a bare-foot, bare-chested king, dust-caked and mad, leaping and dancing, as if before the ark of a holy covenant. Locusts and honey, locusts and honey, fit food for prophets, but I have no clear vision, only expectancy, a void that something will arrive to fulfil, I prophesy it. The grasshoppers leap into the void of the afternoon, not gliding or floating, but hurling themselves, wing-beat by wing-beat, over the plants, their mountaintops, only to sag again on the other side and fall to earth, then hurl themselves again, leaping, leaping, leaping – pht-t-t-t-t, pht-t-t-t-t, pht-t-t-t-t – and I also hurl myself, and I let myself fall, for the joy of falling, tumbling, rolling. I am submerged in the meadow, drowning in locusts and honey, in wisdom and prophesy that cannot be uttered.

There is not the slightest moisture in the grass, the dew long gone, only dryness, summer-afternoon-dryness, time-for-haying-to-be-finished-dryness, dust-in-puffs-as-you-pass-by-dryness, and hot, not humid, but pleasantly, the heat of sun on face and on shoulders. I am covered in the dust by now, caked with it where the sweat of the mow still clings. I wallow in it, in the heat and the sun, lying where I fall, looking up through the orange-red sky of my eyelids, through the chain-lightning blood vessels, back-lit by a long distant sun. I am an offering to the sun, to the heat and dust, to whatever it will bring. The world is my altar stone. I sweat honey and blood together, wetting the dust with my sacrifice, and I take its sacrifice with me too, as I stand and run, a tithe of wetted earth on my skin.

And now the meadow is lost to forest, and I am loosed into the trees like an arrow, piercing its borders, through the whipple-trees and raspberries and arrowwoods, along the cowpath, and beneath the canopy. There is no under-growth, grazed to stubble and trampled to muck, and the black mud, hardened now so late in the summer, holds the shape of cattle hooves, like a bed of fossils. The petri-fied punctures are too round for my naked feet, too hard, so I slow, walk gingerly among them, finding patches of solidity in the midst of them, skirting their edges, where the branches have kept the broad bovine bodies and their soon to be fossilized hoof-prints from approaching the tree trunks. The cow patties, a few days old, are heat-hardened too, but only to a crust, still moist and muddy within, squishing between my toes when I misstep, deliciously, the profoundest proof of God, that even cow dung should feel like this.

The path runs through the woods, running between two fencelines until it reaches the far field along the highway, across from one of the inland lakes, but the void of the afternoon will accept no highways. It opens itself only to the hidden and the forgotten, only to what nature has half-reclaimed, the bones of cattle, green with moss and piled in a pit beyond the cedar rails to my right, a decaying tractor, red more with rust than paint, eyeless and staring, parked finally a few yards beyond the bones, so I scale the fence, sit astride it for a time, savour the moment, not of indecision, but of a decision made and not yet enacted, of knowing what I will do without yet having to do it, then slide down among the green-white bones, among the long ribs and the unrecognizable skulls. These are the portents of what the afternoon anticipates, illegible and obscure. I squat among them, half-naked and smeared with dust, like a madman seeking signs among bones tossed by a giant hand, turning them over in my own hands, reading the omens meant for another, reordering the bones around me, changing who knows what destinies. Only a madman would dare such things, only someone maddened by anticipation, who has seen the very dust wear haloes, who has attended the birth of infant silence, who has drunk the blood and honey of the meadow, who has seen the sun through red chains of lightning.

The bones send me onward without direction, only onward, and I obey, past the tractor, the belts hanging limply and the radiator exposed between its gouged eyes. Whatever trail it made in coming is long overgrown, the skeletal machinery fringed by tall grass, by chokecherry bushes, by young cedars, the growth of several years or more. I run my hand along it as I pass, red paint and red rust, flaking, speckling the grass, staining my fingers, and then there is only forest, birch and maple among the shield ferns. One tree leads to another, always, one to the other, each still believing that there is no end to their leading, one to the other, believing that axes and saws have not yet cut the forest into ribbons, believing that each tree still reaches out to touch another across endless spaces, world without end. I reach my hands too, touching each in turn, and I believe as they do, at least for a time, fall into the eternity that the trees imagine themselves to be, lapse into the forest's long-false but lingering dream of infinity, but a second fenceline, cedar rail, now fallen, dissolves the illusion, as it runs between the woods and a vast, untended field, long untilled.

The trees here do not have the luxury of disbelief.

They are the foot soldiers of war, long in retreat, blow
by blow, furrow by furrow, but now advancing again on
fields gone fallow, their seedlings freely encroaching on
the grain-land, spilling over the fence rails in a long, slow
assault on everything cultivated, leaving the fence hidden
among the newly unrestrained trees and bushes. The
grasses of the field, uncut, come up almost to my chest,
and I leave a trail through them, a wake of bent stalks,
golden, and crushed leaves, verdant, as I make for the
tractor lane across the field, invisible still, but marked
by a double line of trees, a stubborn remnant, so long
besieged by the tilled and the planted, but waiting now,
just a few decades more, to rejoin the wild fecundity of
the forest.

The tractor lane angles away from me, its attendant
trees blocking my view, but I can see a barn behind it.
The doors hang open, and the boards are falling from
the beams, unused, surely, though the lane has not been
abandoned, not wholly, the grass between the ruts shorter
than on either side, and tire tread still showing, dried in
the mud of the last rain. Just a few steps further, and
I can see where the lane ends, not at the settling barn,
but closer, at an old drive shed, barn board too, and
subsiding into its foundations. Its door is ajar, an invi-
tation, and I know that this is what the day has been
expecting, what it birthed in silence and drank in the
meadow and followed among the trees, this, this, this,
but I know not to rush my attendance, know to approach

it slowly, obliquely, as if stalking prey, not raising its suspicions, not causing it alarm, not making my intentions known, until I am right at the door, my hand on the latch, standing at the threshold of possibility, of anticipation, nowhere leading everywhere, nothing holding everything. To pass through this place is to make things come to be, to end possibility, and I hesitate, then step into what is waiting.

There are light-haloed motes of dust like a universe of meteors, quasars, milky ways, supernovas, suspended in their vast distances, their lightyears, between the low beams of the shed. They are the constellations of a fate that might be read if only I knew their language, but I do not read them, only throw myself into them. How many million worlds do I wrench from their orbits as I wade among these stars, send them swirling into the dark corners of the universe, where their lights are blackened, and they settle in the cracks and the pits of the cement slab floor? I am a god, a colossus, striding among the constellations that once foretold my destiny and now foretell nothing. I have scattered the augers, unseated the heavens, left the magi of countless worlds to wonder at the meaning of their night skies.

There, beneath the timbered heavens, the end of what began in the womb of the mow, are two wooden speed boats, almost twins, with long narrow boards sweeping from bow to stern, oval cutouts framing their seats, carefully tarped. They have been here longer than the rusted tractor in the birch forest, longer than the bones bleaching by the split rail fence, tenderly stored and then forgotten beneath the sagging roof and the rotting beams and the galaxies of dust, all this time, unsuspected, awaiting the day, this day, when the labour of the morning would open into an expectancy, when the meadow would intoxicate and the trees lead from one to the other, and place me here, before them, the one who has witnessed the birth of silence, drunk the wine of the meadow, played with the telling-bones of giants, scattered galaxies through the low heavens, and I do not know what they mean, these dry-rotted boats, not at all, only that they were meant for me, with their peeling marine varnish and their worm-eaten wood. They called to me, and I followed, and they are mine.

# About the Author

Jeremy Luke Hill is a husband and father. He teaches literature, makes jams and preserves, reads continental philosophy, uses open source software, watches documentary film, grows trees from seed, and writes poetry, among other things. He keeps a blog at http://vocamus.net/jlh, and he can be reached at jeremylukehill@gmail.com.

www.ingramcontent.com/pod-product-compliance
Lightning Source LLC
Chambersburg PA
CBHW030333020726
47493CB00004B/1254